ORIGINAL AUTHOR
ROBERT LOUIS STEVENSON

ADAPTED BY
CHRIS BAKER

ILLUSTRATED BY
SANTY GUTIÉRREZ

TREASURE ISLAND

Contents

OXFORD
UNIVERSITY PRESS

Chapter 1: The map

My story starts when I was a boy, helping my mother to run the Admiral Benbow Inn. We had a secretive guest ...

I've brought up your meal, Mr Bones.

There's a sailor-man downstairs, sir, so I thought you wouldn't want to come down.

Thank'ee, Jim. Here's fourpence for helpin' me to avoid them sailors.

Mother asks whether you might pay for your room soon, Mr Bones ...

SLAM!

A sound on the stairs made me turn ... it was the sailor-man!

So this is where me old mate Billy Bones is hiding!

Mr Bones and the sailor-man argued.

I'll never give it to you, Black Dog!

The man ran off and Mr Bones collapsed.

Mother! Mother! Mr Bones is ill! Get Doctor Livesey.

Jim! My sea chest ... We mustn't let 'em get ... uuuh ...

The patient's up here, is he?

Yes, sir.

You are not a well man, Billy Bones. You must mend your ways – another rage might kill you.

Billy Bones never really recovered.

Mr Bones ... I brought your food.

Leave it there, boy!

No fourpence for me, let alone any rent for Mother! So much for 'mending your ways,' Billy Bones!

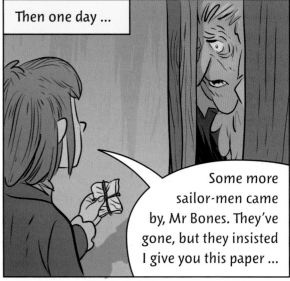

Then one day ...

Some more sailor-men came by, Mr Bones. They've gone, but they insisted I give you this paper ...

The black spot!

Black spot, sir?

It's the pirate summons. They're coming for me. For what's in me sea chest!

Mr Bones! No! You're not well enough to leave.

Uuuh!

Mr Bones? Mr Bones?

Mother! I think Mr Bones has ... died!

We can't be here when the sailors come to take his things. They're violent men!

But he owes us so much money! We can't get by without it. We'll take it from his sea chest first; then we'll go!

We looked in Billy Bones's sea chest …

I'll take what I'm owed, not a penny more.

Mother! Do hurry! They'll be here soon.

Oh, these confusing foreign coins …

Mother! Please hurry!

Are these coins worth sixpence each, do you think? Or more perhaps?

Yes, no! Definitely sixpence each! Just count them quickly!

Just then, something caught my eye in the chest.

Ninety-three … Ninety-four …

Billy Bones, where are ye?

Run!

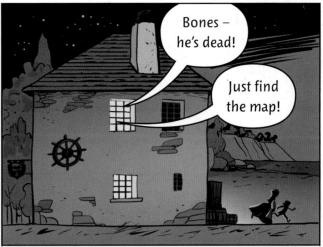

They were after this, sir.

I had better take you to see the squire.

Mother went to stay with friends while I was taken to Squire Trelawney's house. Doctor Livesey was already there.

They were Captain Flint's old pirate crew, sir!

They said they were looking for a map, sir. I think they wanted this!

Doctor! Is this ...?

It's the legendary map showing the location of Captain Flint's hidden treasure!

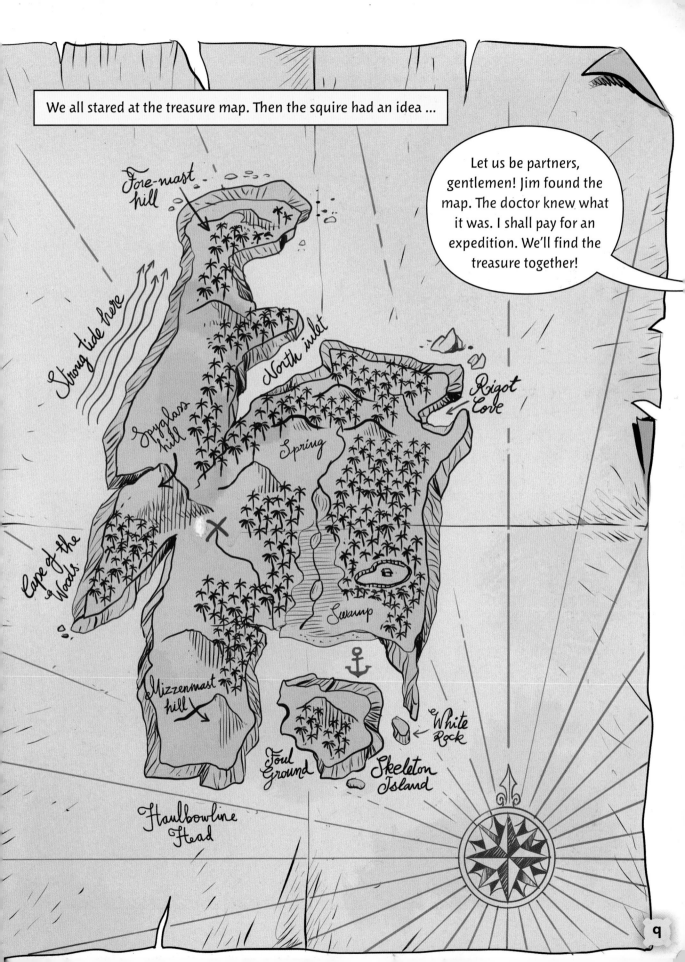

We all stared at the treasure map. Then the squire had an idea ...

Let us be partners, gentlemen! Jim found the map. The doctor knew what it was. I shall pay for an expedition. We'll find the treasure together!

Chapter 2: The mutiny

Squire Trelawney bought a ship, the *Hispaniola*, and hired Captain Smollett to sail it. By chance – or so it seemed – the squire met an old sailor, Long John Silver, who helped him find a crew.

I do think, sirs, that as captain you should have allowed ME to choose the crew!

Don't you approve of the men Long John Silver has already found, Captain Smollett?

Somehow, sir, they make me ... uneasy.

Despite the captain's concerns, we prepared to sail.

We're all ready to sail, Captain Smollett.

Thank you Mr Silver. Weigh anchor!

Aye, aye, sir – off on our treasure hunt!

How does he know about the treasure?

At sea, I helped Long John Silver in the ship's galley.

He told me stories of his adventures at sea ...

... and about his parrot who had once sailed with the pirate, Captain Flint.

Pieces of eight!
Pieces of eight!

We sailed for many uneventful weeks. I lost count of the days. Each day, I had to reach further into the apple barrel for my daily ration of fruit.

Then one day, I overheard the sailors planning something dreadful ...

So why not mutiny now? I'm fed up of those ... *Gentlemen*!

And I keep telling ye – WAIT. Let 'em help us find the treasure, then mutiny!

Why was our old captain, Captain Flint, the greatest pirate ever, eh? Because he could plan. He could wait. Not like yer average pirate.

Squawk! Walk the plank! Dead men don't tell tales!

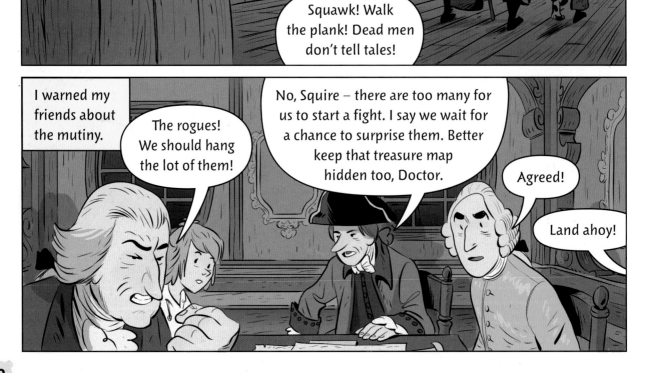

I warned my friends about the mutiny.

The rogues! We should hang the lot of them!

No, Squire – there are too many for us to start a fight. I say we wait for a chance to surprise them. Better keep that treasure map hidden too, Doctor.

Agreed!

Land ahoy!

We had arrived at Treasure Island.

Most of the crew went ashore to get water, and I went too.

The captain, squire and doctor stayed on board. They were looking at an old stockade with interest.

That stockade, gentlemen, looks like a place we might hide out if things start to get nasty.

Meanwhile, on the island, I went off to explore.

Wandering off saved my life, because as I was returning from exploring ...

... Ye've no choice, Tom! Join the mutiny or die! We can't let you blab to the captain!

No! Never! HELP!

BANG! BANG!

ARRRRGH!

What was that?

Gunshot!

Mutiny!

Make for the stockade!

BOOM!

The mutiny had begun sooner than planned. The mutineers still on board the *Hispaniola* weren't ready, and so the captain, doctor and squire were able to escape.

Chapter 3: Jim's adventure

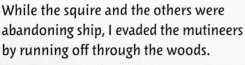

While the squire and the others were abandoning ship, I evaded the mutineers by running off through the woods.

I ran blindly, until I could run no more.

CRACK!

Huh?

Who's there?

I'm poor Ben Gunn. Not seen another human for three long years!

Left me here when we couldn't find the treasure, he did. 'It's no good, we'll never find it without the map,' he said.

I said, 'No, let's keep looking,' but he said, 'You keep looking all you like matey!' And they laughed and marooned me on this island.

Who? Who marooned you?

Long John Silver and his crew!

LONG JOHN SILVER?

Said he'd be back only if he could get the map! You're ... You're not with him, are you?

Long John Silver was in our crew, but he and some men have come ashore and mutinied.

I've made a boat we might use. Come see!

We were looking at the boat when I suddenly heard cannon-fire!

BOOM!

We have to find out what's happened!

We saw my friends retreat to the stockade and raise a flag.

Look, Ben!

I watched helplessly as they fought the mutineers.

Captain Smollett and my other friends are holding them off, but for how long?

BANG!

BANG!

BANG!

Ben? Ben?

The mutineers didn't take the stockade. Some of them were wounded in the battle, so they retreated to make camp.

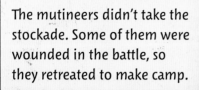

I watched them for a while. I made a guess that they had only left a small crew aboard the *Hispaniola* ...

Fifteen men on a dead man's chest. Yo, ho, ho!

... and that they must have posted guards around the stockade – I didn't dare try to sneak in without a diversion.

I sat there until dark, not knowing what to do. Then suddenly I had what seemed like a great idea ...

Aha! Ben Gunn's boat! I'll row to the *Hispaniola* and cut her adrift!

Then, while they're all running after the *Hispaniola*, I can sneak into the stockade!

It wasn't easy to manage the boat.

I heard two pirates arguing.

You stole it!

No I never!

The pirates began to fight.

Take that!

Arrgh!

The current tugged the ship away. I was knocked backwards.

Ohh!

BANG! BANG!

WHACK!

The next thing I knew, it was morning.

While I was unconscious, I had drifted around the island.

Luckily, the *Hispaniola* was still nearby, having drifted on the same currents.

It's very quiet up on deck.

They've killed each other!

I'm alone, drifting at sea!

It took the day and most of the night to walk to the stockade.

When I got there, I found that the pirates had all gone and nobody was on guard. It was most odd.

They're all asleep! If I were Silver and his lads creeping in on them, they'd be killed before they woke!

Gotcha!

LONG JOHN SILVER?

Oh no! What can we do?

Things look bad, Jim lad. But I've still got a shot in me locker. I'll save ye if you'll put in a good word for me with those friends of yours!

You're going to change sides?

I'm always on the same side – me own! Do we have a deal?

I have no choice. Alright.

Wise lad. Well, they're coming back in!

Now mates! Before you go and elect a new captain, ask yourself a few questions. Who started the mutiny – before I said – by killing Tom? George Merry!

But ...

Who lost the ship? Well, who was guarding it? O'Brien and Hands!

That's true!

Never did trust them two!

BUT, ask yourselves this: who but Long John Silver would have had the brains to get you to this place, take Jim as a hostage, and get that doctor to give me this 'ere treasure map?

How did he get the map?

The treasure!

We'll be rich!

Hooray for Captain Silver!

Trust Long John Silver! Walk the plank!

Later ...

Is he going to double-cross the muntineers – or me? Still, I have no choice but to hope he's brave and clever enough to save us both.

25

Morning Doctor! Come to tend your favourite patients?

Only because a doctor should help any sick man ... even villains like your crew!

Now then, Doctor – I have a friend for ye to meet.

Jim!

Fact is, Doctor, I'm looking to bargain with ye again. On me own behalf. This crew's no use. They'll be cutting each other's throats in a day. If I can join your side, I'll save Jim for ye.

You're a scoundrel, Silver, still I've no choice but to agree.

Silver! What are ye talking to them about?

Doctor, I beached the *Hispaniola* in North Inlet. If you can free me ... and Silver, we might all escape!

Well done, Jim!

The pirates plan to go treasure hunting today ...

Good! We have planned a surprise for them when they find it. Sit tight, and we'll rescue you then!

Chapter 4: Captain Flint's treasure

After the doctor left, we set out to find the treasure.

The map led us to the spot where ...

... the treasure had already been found!

Ho, ho! Very clever, Doctor! You gave me the map yesterday because you'd already found the treasure. Hope you have another trick planned, though, or Jim and I be dead men.

Silver has double-crossed us. I knew it! Get 'em, mates!

Get down, Jim!

The trap was sprung!

BANG! BANG!

That's driven them off for now. Quick! We have to beat them to the boats, or we'll be trapped on this island!

So you see, Silver, Ben Gunn came to our stockade before you and said he'd found the treasure years ago!

When you came to negotiate for the map, I already knew we didn't need it.

Ben had the treasure and plenty of supplies in his cave.

Hero of the story, I am!

Then we found out that you had been captured, Jim.

So we set up our ambush, while Captain Smollett refloated the *Hispaniola*.

Now, then: we must get the treasure on to the *Hispaniola*. Quickly, before those pirates find us!

The treasure!

Help us pack it into bags, Jim.

Just imagine what awful things have been done to get this treasure!

Greed is a terrible thing, Jim. Just take what you can carry.

We sailed away. All of us had to work hard to manage the *Hispaniola* with such a small crew.

Don't leave us behind!

What? Take you on board and risk another mutiny? No thanks!

There are supplies and a share of the treasure in a cave by North Inlet!

We made it to the nearest port. That was where Long John Silver slipped away. He took some of the treasure, but I think we were all pleased to be so cheaply quit of him.

We hired a new crew, and sailed back to England without further adventure.

All of us had an ample share of the treasure and, since we came back, we have used it wisely or foolishly according to our natures.

Captain Smollett has used his share sensibly and retired.

Ben Gunn quickly spent his share in silly ways.

But when his money was all gone, Squire Trelawney kindly gave him a job.

And me? Well, I went on to other adventures ...

Robert Louis Stevenson was born in Edinburgh in 1850. He began writing stories as a child. He studied engineering at college, but he didn't want to be a lighthouse designer like his father and grandfather. Instead, he became a writer. He was often ill with a chest complaint, and he travelled to warm places to try to get better. Eventually he moved to the South Pacific island of Samoa, where he died in 1894. He wrote about forty books in total. Other than *Treasure Island*, the best known are *The Strange Case of Dr Jekyll and Mr Hyde* and *Kidnapped*.

There had been pirate adventure stories before, but *Treasure Island* became the most famous. When people imagine pirates they often think of them much as *Treasure Island* presents them. Long John Silver in particular is a character many people recognize, even if they have not read the book. You can also see influences from *Treasure Island* in many other stories and in films, from *Peter Pan* or *King Solomon's Mines* to *Swallows and Amazons*, and *Pirates of the Caribbean*.